ARE YOU GOING TO BE GOOD?

CARI BEST

PICTURES BY
G. BRIAN KARAS

MELANIE KROUPA BOOKS   Farrar, Straus and Giroux • New York

For my mother—
who would have danced all night, too
                                —C.B.

Text copyright © 2005 by Cari Best
Illustrations copyright © 2005 by G. Brian Karas
Distributed in Canada by Douglas & McIntyre Publishing Group
Color separations by Chroma Graphics PTE Ltd.
Printed and bound in the United States of America by Phoenix Color Corporation
Book design by Nancy Goldenberg
First edition, 2005
10 9 8 7 6 5 4 3 2 1

www.fsgkidsbooks.com

Library of Congress Cataloging-in-Publication Data
Best, Cari.
       Are you going to be good? / Cari Best ; pictures by G. Brian Karas.— 1st ed.
            p.   cm.
       Summary: While Robert is attending his first "night party" to celebrate Great-Gran Sadie's 100th
       birthday, his manners disappoint family members and relatives but please the guest of honor, who
       loves his dance steps.
       ISBN-13: 978-0-374-30394-5
       ISBN-10: 0-374-30394-0
       [1. Parties—Fiction.   2. Etiquette—Fiction.   3. Old age—Fiction.]   I. Karas, G. Brian, ill.   II. Title.

PZ7.B46579Ar 2005
[E]—dc22

                                                                                            2004046945

It is dark outside. Almost pajama time. But Robert is not going to bed. Mama and Daddy and big sister Alice are going to a party.

And Robert is going, too.

1, 2, 3, 4, 5, 6, 7, 8, 9, 10, 11, 12, 13, 14, 15,

Robert puts on his socks. And his new shirt. There are pearly buttons on the ends of his sleeves. This is his going-to-a-party tie. And these are his clean ears and neck.

"Who is the party for?" asks Robert.

And Daddy answers, "The party is for Great-Gran Sadie. She is one hundred years old today."

"I can count to a hundred," says Robert. And he does.

"Good boy," says Mama.

Robert gets dressed up just like his daddy. He has a handkerchief in his pocket.
And shoes without scratches that he and Daddy polish till they shine.

"I like getting dressed up," says Robert.

"Are you going to dance tonight?" asks Alice as she combs Robert's hair.

"Are you going to eat tonight?" asks Daddy as he closes his coat.

"Are you going to be good tonight?" asks Mama as she kisses his nose.

"Yes! Yes! Yes!" says Robert, jumping up and down.

There is a present for Great-Gran Sadie in the hall. But Robert would like to give her his own. He counts out exactly one hundred sweet cherry berries, and carefully wraps them in his handkerchief.

"Now I'm ready," he says.

In the car, they practice "Please." They practice "Thank you" and "Excuse me," too. In the car, they sing and laugh and ride for miles on their way to the party—the party for Great-Gran Sadie, who is one hundred years old today.

"Remember not to mumble," says Alice. "Or talk too loud," she adds. "Some old people aren't good at hearing. And some just like it quiet."

"And never interrupt," says Daddy. "Some old people expect perfect manners."

"No running or jumping," says Mama. "Some old people are very breakable."

"Okay. Okay. Okay," says Robert, covering his ears. "I'll remember everything."

Soon Alice says, "Here we are!"
And Daddy says, "Right on time!"
Mama says, "Be a good boy!"
And Robert says, "Let's go!"

There are lights at the party, and music and flowers and lots of big people.

"Excuse me," says Robert as he bumps into one.

Daddy is in charge. First they walk. Then they talk. Robert shakes a lot
of hands.

"You know Cousin Sidney," says Daddy. "Say 'Hi' to Uncle Phil. Remember
Aunt Aggie?"

Robert doesn't. But he says "Hi" anyway. "Which one is Great-Gran Sadie?"
he asks.

And Daddy answers, "She isn't here yet. Some old people take a long time to
get ready."

There is a lot of food to choose from. And Robert is very hungry. He tastes some things. And puts some back.

"Don't do that," whispers Daddy.

So Robert puts the things in his pocket.

Robert has never seen so many drinks. He tries a few. And spits some out.

"Don't do that," whispers Aunt Aggie.

So Robert pours the rest in the flowers.

The sound of the splashing reminds Robert that he has something

important to do. But Daddy is still walking and talking and shaking hands.

Robert waits and waits. Finally he goes to the men's room by himself.
On the way out, he tries the fancy soap.
"Don't do that," whispers Cousin Sidney.
So Robert makes monkey faces in the mirror.

Back at the party, Great-Gran Sadie has arrived. She has pointy shoes and bony fingers and eyes as round as Cheerios. Robert thinks she looks like the bird that comes to their window back home.

"Hello, little man," she says.

Robert peeks out from behind Daddy. He is not sure whether to whisper or to shout or to shake her one-hundred-year-old hand. So he smiles at her knees and at the points of her shoes and follows Daddy to the dinner table.

"Would you like some salad?" the waiter asks.

"Yes, please," says Robert. And Mama beams.

But when the salad comes, it has olives and peppers and cheese that smells like someone's feet. Robert holds his nose.

"Don't do that," whispers Grandpa Jack.

So Robert plays monster mash on his plate.

"What's for dessert?" he asks. But no one is listening.

Then the chicken comes. And it has mushrooms that he can't pick out. And onions and garlic and french fried zucchini.

"What's for dessert?" Robert asks again. But this time, he doesn't wait for an answer.

Under the table, Robert sees Daddy's shoes, Mama's shoes, Alice's, and some others he's never seen before.

Then he sees the pointy ones.

"I know you," he says. "How about a happy birthday shine!"

"Don't do that," whispers Alice.

So Robert crawls back to his chair.

Then, while Grandpa Jack makes a speech and Aunt Ida makes a speech, Robert draws a picture.

"Don't do that," whispers Uncle Phil.

So Robert builds an igloo with everybody's ice.

Then Uncle Harry makes a speech and Cousin Gertrude makes a speech.

So Robert plays a throwing game: How many olives can I get in Mama's water glass?

"Don't do that," she whispers.

Robert looks all around the room. Is this what a night party is all about?
First you stand. Then you sit. Then you yawn. And then you sleep.

Then, just when Robert decides he's ready to go home, someone says,
"It's time to dance!"

"I like to dance," says Robert.

The music starts slowly,
and then it gets faster.

Robert starts slowly, and
then *he* gets faster, too.
He wiggles and he jiggles.
He quivers and he quakes.

Robert feels like
a firecracker
ready to explode.

"Don't do that," whispers Daddy.
"Don't do that," whispers Mama.
"Don't do that," whisper Alice and
all the other relatives.

All except Great-Gran Sadie, her toes tapping to the music.
"DO THAT AGAIN!" she says.

Then, to everyone's surprise, she kicks off her pointy shoes and starts to dance, too. She wiggles and she jiggles. She quivers and she quakes.

"Yippee!" she shouts.

Soon the music stops. And so do the two dancers. Great-Gran Sadie laughs with tears that just keep coming. Suddenly, Robert remembers his handkerchief.

"Here," he says, forgetting all about the one hundred sweet cherry berries.

"Uh-oh," says Robert as the berries come tumbling out.

But when Great-Gran Sadie says, "These are my very favorite candies!" Robert laughs, too.

"Have one," he says.

And when dessert finally comes, Great-Gran Sadie *and* Robert blow out all one hundred candles, while Mama and Daddy, big sister Alice, and all the other relatives clap and cheer and sing the birthday song.

"I can't wait till next year," says Robert.
"Neither can I," says Great-Gran Sadie.
And they dance one more dance before it's time to go home.